Moriah the Strongheart

by John Rawson

illustrated by Will Sweeney

✦ Prologue ✦

Long ago in the Kingdom of Kurk, the good king died and an evil Overlord took his place. Powerful and merciless, the Overlord bent people to his bidding and robbed them of their will. To this day, no one knows how. This wicked man drained the land of hope, until the world itself grew colorless and gray. Only the Stronghearts could resist him, and for too many years, they were scattered and few.

Hidden

Moriah shuffled through the marketplace, head down. She edged past two soldiers, who seemed to be inspecting every person who passed. *Coming here was a mistake*, she thought as she pulled her hood tighter around her face.

She had expected a spy or two, observing from the shadows. She was unprepared for the soldiers.

Had she rubbed enough gray ash on her skin? Was the hood of her cloak hiding the shine of her hair? She prayed no one would notice that she was a Strongheart.

Only the Stronghearts thought for themselves. Only the Stronghearts felt the yearning for freedom. Most of the people of Kurk acted like they were sleepwalking. They were in a fog. Some Stronghearts could awaken the spirit in others, just by touching them. But this was dangerous. If a Strongheart was caught, he just...disappeared.

Her grandmother had taught Moriah to be careful. "Keep your eyes to the ground and your thoughts off your face," she had warned. "And whatever you do, touch no one. Touch nothing."

Going into the village was a terrible risk. Nan forbade such a venture. But Moriah could no longer bear cowering in their remote cottage, pretending to be as gray and colorless as the land. She'd come to search for other Stronghearts.

Instead, she saw gray villagers, shuffling about their business with their heads down. Few glanced up. Those who did had dull eyes and lifeless faces.

Moriah turned down a side street and breathed a sigh of relief. Fewer gray shufflers. And no soldiers!

Then she tripped on her cloak.

As Moriah stumbled, hands caught her, lifting her back onto her feet.

She raised her eyes to a tall youth, his hands still clutching hers. The youth's gray pallor brightened and his eyes slowly cleared, like someone waking from a long sleep.

The young man blinked, looking surprised. "What did you do to me?" he asked.

Moriah remembered her grandmother's warnings and pulled away from him. But not wanting to appear rude, she smiled. "I did nothing. 'Tis you who did something. Thank you for catching me!"

As she spoke, she studied the youth. His tunic was colorless like hers, but of fine fabric. An unusual dagger was thrust in his belt—a dagger with a pale, gray-green blade.

The boy stared at Moriah. "I have never met anyone like you," he murmured. "But I have heard...."

He said no more. Instead, he plucked a flower from the edge of the road and offered it to Moriah. As she took the stem in her fingers, the gray blossom turned vivid scarlet. Moriah froze. She knew that some Stronghearts brought color to whatever they touched. Nan wore gloves for just that reason. But it had never happened with her before

The boy blinked, and then he slowly smiled. "So you are a...."

"Rebel!"

The voice snapped like a whip. The flower fell from Moriah's hands, and the tall boy wilted to gray.

Moriah whirled to see who frightened her new friend so. Only then did she remember. *Head down. Dull eyes. Empty thoughts.*

It was too late.

From atop a horse, a tall man, shimmering with power and flanked by soldiers, looked down. The Overlord.

"So, Daran," he said. "You caught a Strongheart my soldiers missed. Well done! Now crush the flower."

Moriah felt weak fingers clutch at her sleeve. "I never...." Daran began.

The Overlord studied Moriah through narrowed eyes. "And who might you be?"

Moriah stared up at him, silent, defiant.

He nodded once. "Nan Cooper's brat, more than likely. I've long suspected her." Then he commanded, "*Seize the Strongheart!*"

Moriah turned to flee. But Daran's hand was still on her sleeve, and she caught a glimpse of his eyes, pleading. Without thinking, she grabbed his wrist and pulled him along. All around them, villagers scattered in every direction.

Moriah wove between carts and food stalls, while the soldiers struggled to maneuver their horses through the crowded street. She plucked up tomatoes, then eggs and grapes, and hurled them at the soldiers. Each touch of her hand restored color. Soon the men were splattered with red, yellow, and purple.

Still the soldiers came after them, leaping from their horses. Moriah knocked over a stack of wooden cages, releasing a flock of chickens that squawked and fluttered in the faces of the soldiers.

"Quick!" Moriah pulled the boy behind a stall, then through the narrow space between two huts. They raced through a maze of alleys. On the edge of the village, Moriah found a path that went deep into the woods. She beckoned the boy to hurry.

✦ Hunted ✦

Before they had run far, Daran fell to the ground. "Please," he wheezed. "We must rest a moment."

"No," Moriah cried. "He knows about Nan." But she, too, doubled over and gasped for breath.

Daran struggled to his knees. "You are both Stronghearts, you and your nan."

"We are," Moriah said. "But I know so little about what that means. Nan never wanted me to.... Oh, we must warn her." She reached out to Daran and they ran.

As they neared Moriah's cottage, Daran slowed the pace. Moriah tried to pull away. "We must hurry," she scolded.

"Hush," Daran warned. "Listen."

From the edge of the woods near the cottage, Moriah heard shouts. Soldiers burst from the cottage door, dragging an old woman with them.

Moriah started toward them, but Daran grabbed her, pulling her back into the shelter of the trees. Though she struggled, he held her tightly. The soldiers threw her grandmother across the back of a horse and rode away.

Only after the soldiers were gone did Daran let her go. Moriah turned on the boy. "Why did you stop me?" Then her eyes narrowed in rage. "You *wanted* Nan to get caught."

He shook his head. "Listen. If you are caught too, you cannot do anything," he said. "They will lock you up with the others."

"The others?"

"The other Stronghearts. The Overlord cannot tolerate any of you," Daran explained. "Having watched you in the market place, I well understand why. Your color angers him to the edge of madness. Your spirit of independence, too."

Moriah paid him little attention. Her thoughts were swirling. "If there are so many of us, we could come together and rescue...."

But Daran was shaking his head again. "Whenever soldiers find Stronghearts, they throw them in the castle's dungeon."

Moriah stared at the young man. "How do you know all this?"

The young man looked down. "I...I live at the castle. I was...I am the prince."

"The prince!" Moriah exclaimed. "And you let this happen?"

"I was but a babe when my parents died," Daran said. "And you've met my uncle, the Overlord." He shuddered. "He is not an easy man to argue with."

But Moriah was hardly listening. "A dungeon full of Stronghearts. We must rescue Nan and the others at once!" She pointed at Daran, who straightened. "Prince Daran, lead the way!"

Daran was little help at first. His uncle's influence had made his mind slow and dull. But Moriah pointed out they could follow the horses' tracks to the road. And it was Daran, when they came to a fork in the road, who found a single turquoise bead.

"Oh, Nan, brilliant Nan!" Moriah sang, close to tears. "She has left a trail for us." Moriah kissed the bead. "This bead is from a necklace Nan used to keep alive my memory of color."

As Moriah and Daran traveled, they collected more beads dropped at each crossroad. It was clear the soldiers were taking Nan to the castle. As they traveled, Moriah was careful not to let her fingers touch any living thing, or else its color would mark their path.

Many times they had to duck into the forest as travelers or bands of soldiers passed.

Finally they stopped to rest and eat. As Moriah bent over a stream to drink, the grass bloomed green beneath her fingers. At that moment, she heard approaching hoofbeats. Soldiers!

"They will see the color!" Moriah cried to Daran. "We must hide!"

Daran leaped up. "No time," he said. "Wrap your hands in your cloak and climb that tree. I will run a little farther down the road and go out to them. If they have me, they'll not look for you."

"You cannot!"

"It is the only way," he insisted. He pulled the dagger from his belt and handed it to Moriah. "This may help you. Quickly now, before they are upon us!"

Moriah watched from the tree as the soldiers surrounded Daran, then rode off with him.

◆ Alone ◆

Long after the soldiers were gone, Moriah huddled in the tree, clutching Daran's dagger. The journey to the castle seemed hopeless without him. The Overlord snatched every Strongheart up, one by one. What could one girl do alone?

Yet she could not go back to Nan's cottage and her old gray life. And she couldn't abandon Nan or Daran or the imprisoned Stronghearts. *At least I have Daran's dagger*, she thought, looking down at it.

Her eyes widened. Pale no more, it gleamed bright jade green. Then she looked around her with amazement—and horror. The tree she'd been sitting in was brilliantly colored—and blossoming.

Down she climbed and away she ran. When she was safely distant, she pulled her cloak around her and began shuffling along the road. She kept her eyes down, not only to act the part of dull traveler, but to watch for more beads.

This was not a busy road. Mostly soldiers passed by, but mixed with them were a few farmers and merchants, dragging their wares to the castle. Moriah joined a cluster of farmers, shambling along.

But when she saw a clutch of colored beads, all in a pile, she stopped short. Why so many beads? Why here?

She looked up and was surprised to see the castle so close, yet separated from her by a deep gorge. The road, which swung down the steep hill, was lined with soldiers who inspected every passerby. She knew then that the beads were a warning.

A woodcutter with a load of logs bumped into her. "You're blocking the way," he grumbled.

"Sorry," she said, lifting her eyes to his.

Blue eyes met green. Both startled, they quickly ducked their heads.

"You were in the marketplace," the woodcutter whispered.

"Yes, and now...." Moriah began.

"Hush!" the woodcutter warned. He waved at a narrow path beside the road. "There is a footbridge," he said. "Fly!"

The woodcutter walked on. Moriah slipped off the road and onto the path. Out of sight of the road, she ran.

Rescue?

Moments later, she came to a mile-deep gorge spanned by a slender rope bridge. Her hands shook, but she grasped the rope and took a step. Soon she was dangling over the chasm. She had not gone far when she heard shouts. Soldiers! The wooden slats shook as they started after her.

She clung to the rope rail and forced herself on, faster, step by step, as the bridge swayed and shimmied, making her stomach clench. She was almost to the other side when she looked back. A line of soldiers was partway across.

Panting, Moriah pulled out the dagger, lifted
it high for them to see, and began sawing at the
rope. She heard a panicked shout. The blade did
its work quickly. The first rope gave as the
soldiers scrambled back. The second followed. As
the bridge fell, Moriah turned and ran up the path
to the castle.

The castle towers looked as if they had been carved out of the mountain itself. Moriah watched from behind a tree until she saw a crowd of gray-clad servants unloading wagons near one tower. She crept to a wagon, heaved a sack over her shoulder, and joined the plodding line. One servant raised his head a moment to meet her eye, then gave a nod. Yet another Strongheart!

Moriah lowered her sack onto a pile in the kitchen and then ducked through an open doorway. No one followed.

She crept along, searching for a way to the dungeon. There were many soldiers and guards, but she dodged every one by slipping down a stairway or turning a corner.

At last she came to a hallway leading to a small room.

And there she saw the prince.

"Daran!" Moriah exclaimed as she ran into the room. "I'm so glad I've found you. Luck is with me! Please, show me the way to the dungeon. I have your...."

Daran stood, stooped and gray. "I know you," he said dully. "Don't I know her, Uncle?" Moriah stared at Daran in confusion. Then she spun around and was face-to-face with the Overlord.

"My soldiers are not so blind that they'd miss seeing you in castle hallways." He smiled unpleasantly. "No, you were herded here. I thought Daran might like the honor of locking you up. Daran?"

"Yes, Uncle," Daran said. He held out a hand to Moriah. "But first, return the dagger you stole from me."

Moriah reared back, indignant. "Stole?" she snapped.

"And my beads," Daran said, barely emphasizing *my*.

Moriah looked at him more carefully. Gray he might be, but there was a glimmer in his eyes. She *hoped* she saw a glimmer. "I have no choice," Moirah said as she bowed her head.

"No choice at all," the Overlord said, gloating, as two soldiers moved into the small room.

Moriah drew out the dagger, shockingly green.

At the sight of its brightness, the Overlord gasped and threw his arm up across his eyes. Daran reached out, not for the dagger, but for her hand.

But her hand was full of Nan's beads, which she threw at the Overlord, blasting him with color.

He backed away, cursing, stumbling into the soldiers. While color awakened some, it wounded him to the quick.

"Quickly," Daran said. And they ran down the hallway.

The two soldiers gave chase. Moriah was ready to slash at them with the dagger, but a gray-haired servant spilled a sack full of candles in the hallway. The soldiers tripped and went down.

More guards followed, but a green-eyed woodcutter dropped an armful of logs and blocked their way.

Daran and Moriah plunged down a stone stairway to the very bottom of the castle. There, behind a heavy door, was the dungeon.

"The dagger," Daran gasped. "It will open the door."

"You do it," Moriah said, holding out the knife.

Daran wouldn't take it. "It will fade in my hands," he said. "You must do it."

Moriah lifted the dagger, plunged the blade into the keyhole, and turned. There was a clank and the door burst open, pushed from within.

Moriah was surrounded by brilliantly colorful people—Stronghearts! And there in the crowd was Nan, beaming.

"Follow me!" someone cried. The Stronghearts swarmed up the stairway of the castle, touching every soldier and servant they encountered. Hope, it seemed, was making them stronger. And their numbers swelled as they went.

Suddenly a new force of strength and joy surged through the castle. Even the Overlord was not strong enough to withstand it. As the Stronghearts broke into his chambers, he lifted a sword to fight, then dropped it again just as quickly, shielding his eyes and screaming in pain at their touch. His hold on power broken, he fled. No one knew or cared where he went.

❦ Epilogue ❦

*Prince Daran was quickly crowned
by a council of Stronghearts, the
people he appointed as advisors.
As King Daran, he ordered a
procession to spread the news of the
kingdom's release from the Overlord.*

*Moriah and Nan rode with
Daran down the mountain and
through the kingdom, touching every
living thing they passed.*

Behind them...

. . . a wave of color flowed like a river.